Mason Crest
450 Parkway Drive, Suite D
Broomall, PA 19008
www.masoncrest.com
Developed and produced by Mason Crest

© 2017 by Mason Crest, an imprint of National Highlights, Inc. All rights reserved. No part of this publication may be reproduced or transmitted in any form or by any means, electronic or mechanical, including photocopying, recording, taping, or any information storage and retrieval system, without permission from the publisher.

Printed and bound in the United States of America.

First printing
9 8 7 6 5 4 3 2 1

Series ISBN: 978-1-4222-3538-6
ISBN: 978-1-4222-3543-0
ebook ISBN: 978-1-4222-8363-9

Images
Cover: SeanPavonePhoto/Dollarphoto.
Art Directors & TRIP Photo Library/Malcolm Lee: 14b; Gail Mooncy/CORBIS 37t;
Bettmann/CORBIS 41tl; Robert Harding Picture Library: 13t, 13b, 18t, 39b, 42b; Nan Melville: 34b; Peter Newark's American Pictures: 8t, 9b, 9t, 10b, 11t, 26t, 27t, 35t, 40b; North Wind Picture Archives: 8b, 10t, 24t, 40t; Rex Features: SteveWood 11 b; 36t, 38t, 38t, 38b, 41cr, 41 bl, David Rentas 43cl ;Frank Spooner Pictures: 11b, 12t, 17b, 27b, 39t; Dreamstime: Palinchak 4t, Kropic 26b, Ritu Jethani 33c, Rolf52 35b, Ffooter 39t, Rob Corbett 39b, Songquan Deng 42t, David Mellan 42b; John Angelillo/UPI/Newscom 27c; JDG/Freeimageslive: 37t;
Laurence Agron, 43b.

Library of Congress Cataloging-in-Publication data is on file with the publisher.

Words in **bold** are explained in the glossary on pages 46 and 47.

MAJOR
World Cities

BEIJING
BERLIN
LONDON
MOSCOW
NEW YORK
PARIS
ROME
SYDNEY

CONTENTS

Introduction	4-5
Maps of the city	6-7
New York's early history	8-9
After the Revolution	10-11
The people of New York	12-13
Buildings and bridges	14-15
Open spaces	16-17
Homes and housing	18-19
Education	20-21
Religion	22-23
Industry and finance	24-25
Crime and punishment	26-27
Getting around	28-29
Shops and markets	30-31
Food and drink	32-33
Entertainment	34-35
Museums and galleries	36-37
Special events	38-39
City characters	40-41
The future of New York	42-43
Timeline	44-45
Glossary	46-47
Index	48

INTRODUCTION

New York City is on the east coast of the US in the southeastern corner of New York State. It has a population of more than eight million, the most of any city in the country, and an area of 302 square miles (783 sq km). Four of its boroughs (Manhattan, Staten Island, Brooklyn, and Queens) are completely or partly on islands in the Hudson River, East River and New York Bay. Most of the fifth, the Bronx, is on the mainland.

The Big Apple

"The Big Apple" was a term probably first used by jazz musicians to mean any large city. Now the nickname refers only to New York, with its unique style and energy. New Yorkers often claim that their city's lively streets, busy shops, excellent cultural life, and dynamic financial district make it the most exciting place on Earth. The New York skyline, with its sleek skyscrapers, is a worldwide symbol of big city life.

▲ Many gleaming skyscrapers, full of offices and apartments, tower over New York. This unique skyline is instantly recognizable to other people all over the world.

Grid system

People can find their way around easily in New York because most of the city's roads are built on a grid system. Numbered streets run from right to left and numbered avenues go up and down. There are some exceptions to this rule, for example the famous road called Broadway, which runs diagonally across much of Manhattan.

4

Major World Cities

FAST FACTS
NEW YORK

STATUS
Most populous city in the US; headquarters of the United Nations

AREA
302 sq miles (783 sq km)

POPULATION
8.4 million (2013)

GOVERNING BODY
Elected mayor, borough presidents, and city council

CLIMATE
Average temperatures range from 26 F (-3°C) in January to 84 F (29°C) in July

TIME ZONE
Eastern Standard Time

CURRENCY
US Dollar ($); 1 dollar = 100 cents

OFFICIAL LANGUAGE
English

A multicultural city

New York has always been home to people of many nationalities. Now old-established Irish, Italian, Jewish and African-American communities mingle with groups who have arrived more recently from places such as Honduras and El Salvador. In areas such as Chinatown, members of the same race live together. Elsewhere, languages and lifestyles mix to make New York a truly multicultural city.

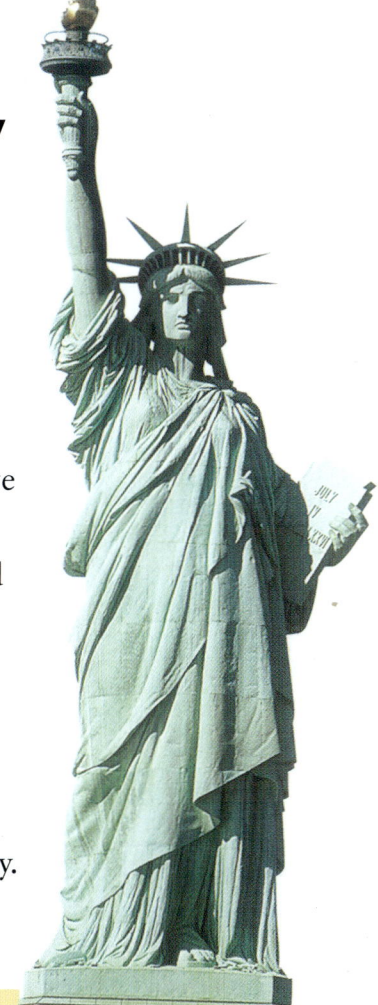

➤ The Statue of Liberty is the most famous symbol of New York. It was made in France then shipped to New York and unveiled in 1886.

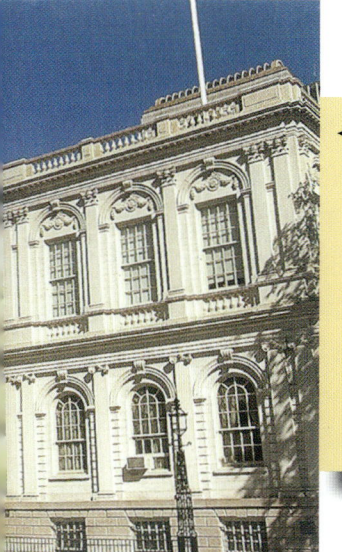

◀ City Hall, in south Manhattan. This is where the mayor works and where public events and celebrations are sometimes held.

City government

New York City is governed by an elected mayor, whose offices are in City Hall and whose official residence is Gracie Mansion. The mayor is assisted by five borough presidents, a 51-member council, and a huge staff. New York also houses the headquarters of the **United Nations**, which overlooks the East River.

MAPS OF THE CITY

These maps show New York as it is today. The area map shows all five New York boroughs and the surrounding region. The street map gives a close-up view of Manhattan borough, the heart of New York City. Many of the places mentioned in the book are marked.

NEW YORK BOROUGHS

1. Staten Island
2. Manhattan
3. Brooklyn
4. Queens
5. The Bronx

① Statue of Liberty. Liberty Island
② Museum of Immigration. Ellis Island
③ Battery Park
④ Ground Zero
⑤ Financial District
⑥ Wall Street
⑦ South Street Seaport
⑧ Brooklyn Bridge
⑨ City Hall
⑩ Chinatown
⑪ Little Italy
⑫ SoHo
⑬ Lower East Side
⑭ Flatiron Building
⑮ Greenwich Village
⑯ Chelsea
⑰ Empire State Building
⑱ Garment District
⑲ Chelsea
⑳ Theater District
㉑ Times Square
㉒ Rockefeller Center
㉓ Grand Central Terminal
㉔ Chrysler Building
㉕ United Nations St
㉖ St. Patrick's Cathedral
㉗ Museum of Modern Art
㉘ Lincoln Center
㉙ Central Park
㉚ Fifth Avenue
㉛ Metropolitan Museum of Art
㉜ Dakota Building
㉝ American Museum of Natural History
㉞ Gracie Mansion
㉟ Guggenheim Museum
㊱ El Barrio
㊲ Cathedral of St John the Divine
㊳ Harlem

6　　　　　　　　　　　　　　　　　　　　　　　　　　　　　　　Major World Cities

NEW YORK

7

NEW YORK'S EARLY HISTORY

The first inhabitants of the area where New York now lies were Native Americans. They belonged to tribes of the **Algonquian** nation and later also of the **Iroquois**. Their traditional ways of life changed after Europeans settled in the region in the 17th century.

▲ This village, made up of wooden **longhouses**, belonged to the Algonquian Wappinger tribe. They lived on Manhattan Island before the arrival of the Dutch in the 17th century.

Early exploration

In 1524 the Italian explorer Giovanni da Verrazzano sailed along America's east coast and became the first European to see the future site of New York. In 1609 Englishman Henry Hudson landed on Manhattan Island, then sailed 150 miles (240 km) down the river later named after him. Hudson worked for a trading organization called the Dutch West India Company. In 1624 the company set up the Dutch **colony** of New Netherlands in the area that Hudson had explored.

New Amsterdam

Many Dutch families settled in the New Netherlands area. In 1625 some moved to the southern end of Manhattan Island and founded a town called New Amsterdam. A year later, Dutchman Peter Minuit became governor of the town. Minuit then bought Manhattan from the Native Americans for cloth and beads.

▲ The Dutch city of New Amsterdam in 1659. Its buildings included a church (center) and a windmill (far left).

Major World Cities

Peter Stuyvesant

During the 17th century, people settled in areas around Manhattan that later became the four other boroughs of New York City. At the same time, New Amsterdam spread north. In 1646 Peter Stuyvesant became the stern new governor of the town. He made it a city in 1653 and built a wooden defensive wall along its northern edge. Wall Street, in New York's Financial District now marks the place where the wall stood.

New York

The British had colonies in North America and wanted New Amsterdam too, so in 1664 they sent four warships to seize the city. They succeeded easily as the Dutch West India Company did not defend the colony. The inhabitants of New Amsterdam did not oppose the British either, as they hated the strict laws that Peter Stuyvesant had passed. The British renamed the city New York after James, Duke of York, the brother of British King Charles II.

▲ Peter Stuyvesant improved the New Amsterdam settlement in many ways, including building its first hospital and adding paved roads.

▲ In 1783, when the defeated British troops had left New York, George Washington entered the city in triumph.

The American Revolution

Many New Yorkers and other Americans did not want to be ruled by a British government far away in London. In 1775 they began a revolution, led by **George Washington**, to end British rule. In 1776 the British won several battles in New York. They took over the city, but were defeated elsewhere and in 1783 gave up their North American colonies. In 1789, New York City became the capital of the newly formed US and Washington was sworn in there as the country's first president.

NEW YORK 9

AFTER THE REVOLUTION

In 1790 Philadelphia took over as the American capital. But New York still grew amazingly fast—in ten years the population rose by 30,000 to reach 79,000 in 1800. This growth continued throughout the 19th century and beyond.

Growth and change

In 1811 a new plan for the city was devised that divided the land above 14th Street into a grid. This still forms the basis of Manhattan's layout. Another important event was the opening of the Erie Canal in 1825. Goods for shipping overseas were brought along the canal to New York, which grew into a major seaport. In 1842 the Croton **Aqueduct** brought pure water to the city for the first time. Then in 1858 Central Park was laid out. This was the largest park in the country.

▲ The 363-mile (585 m)-long, 30-foot-wide Erie Canal was built in just seven years. It linked New York's Hudson River to the **Great Lakes**.

New arrivals

From the 1820s, thousands of European **immigrants** poured into New York City. The pace of immigration grew faster in mid-century, after famine in Ireland and revolution in Germany led people to seek refuge abroad. Immigrant numbers increased further still in the 1880s, when Jews escaping ill-treatment in Eastern Europe and Russia arrived in the city. Poor Italians also came to New York looking for work.

◄ Immigrants at Ellis Island in 1900. People arriving there had to have a medical examination. If they were suffering from an infectious disease, they were sent back home.

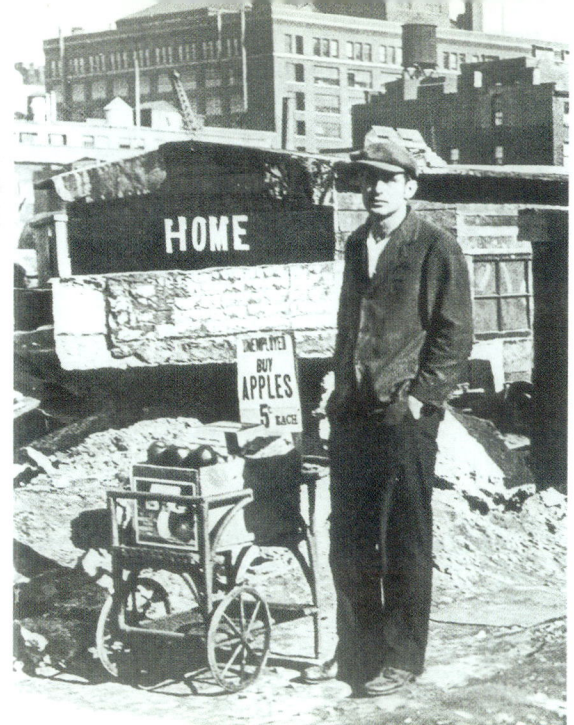

▲ About 25 percent of New Yorkers were unemployed in the 1930s depression. They sold their belongings to make money, but many people lost their homes and had to live in **shantytowns**.

The Civil War and after

From 1861 to 1865 the North of the USA, including New York, took part in a **Civil War** against the South. There was not much fighting in the city, although race riots broke out in 1863, mainly between Irish and black Americans. The North won the war and New York thrived again, but its government was controlled by the corrupt **Tammany Society**. The society became less powerful after its leader, William Marcy Tweed, was imprisoned in 1873.

The 20th century

In the late 19th century New York covered little more than Manhattan Island. Then in 1898 it joined Queens, Brooklyn, Staten Island, and the Bronx to form Greater New York, the modern city. As the 20th century began, skyscrapers sprang up and the city boomed. The boom ended in 1929 when the **Wall Street Crash** brought economic **depression**. New York slowly recovered and after **World War II** more immigrants flooded in, many from Puerto Rico.

September 11, 2001

New York has faced many problems since the 1950s. In 1964 there were race riots in Harlem, and in 1975 the city went bankrupt. But on September 11, 2001, New York endured its worst tragedy yet. In the morning of that day, Arab terrorists flew two passenger aeroplanes into the World Trade Center. By 10:30 a.m. both of its towers had collapsed, and about 2,800 people, including more than 300 firefighters, were dead. Despite their grief, New Yorkers were determined that their city would recover.

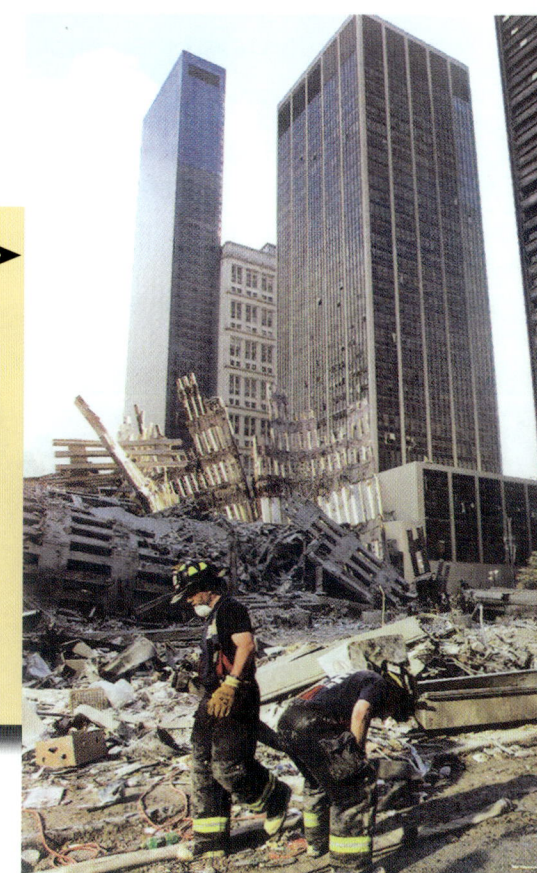

Two firefighters ▶ stumble through the wreckage of the World Trade Center. Hundreds of them rushed to the scene when the south tower fell. Many were then killed when the north tower collapsed.

NEW YORK

THE PEOPLE OF NEW YORK

The population of New York has contained members of many races ever since the 17th century. Now about 40 percent of its inhabitants are immigrant**s** or have parents who were.

The Irish

Thousands of Irish people came to New York in the mid-19th century when famine hit Ireland. Many settled in an area of Manhattan called Hell's Kitchen, where they lived in poverty. Now the city's Irish population is huge—more Irish people live in New York than in Dublin. They organize one of the most exciting events of the year, the St. Patrick's Day Parade.

Little Italy

Thousands of Italians emigrated to New York from the late 19th century. Most settled in Manhattan's Lower East Side, in an area that became known as Little Italy. There they lived in crowded **tenements**, opened Italian restaurants, and held Italian festivals. Now most New York Italians live in the Belmont area of the Bronx, but Little Italy has kept its unique style.

▲ New Yorkers from many backgrounds live side by side. Here all kinds of people mingle at Coney Island Beach.

New York's Jews

Jews moved into the Lower East Side at about the same time as Italians. There they built synagogues and opened shops selling **kosher** food. Many Jews still live in the area, but others have moved out of Manhattan. There is now a large community of **Hasidic Jews** in the Crown Heights area of Brooklyn.

◀ **Orthodox** Jews stroll through Chinatown. The boy in the front of the picture wears the traditional Jewish *yarmulke* (skullcap).

Major World Cities

Chinatown

Many Chinese men first went to the USA to find work mining gold and building railroads. By the 1880s about 10,000 had moved to New York. Most lived in the Chinatown area of the Lower East Side, to the south of Little Italy. Now over 200,000 Chinese people live there. Its streets are lined with restaurants as well as antique shops, Chinese medicine centers, and **Buddhist** temples.

PUERTO RICANS

About a quarter of New Yorkers are **Latinos**. Many came from Puerto Rico, a Caribbean island that has been part of the US since 1899. During the 1950s, the US government encouraged Puerto Ricans to move to New York. Some settled in the southeast of Harlem, known as Spanish Harlem or El Barrio. Others moved into Manhattan's West Side. Gang warfare there between Puerto Ricans and non-Puerto Ricans inspired the musical *West Side Story* by Leonard Bernstein.

▲ Shoppers in New York's Chinatown. Food stores in this area sell all kinds of ingredients for Chinese cooking, such as fish, noodles, and bamboo shoots.

African Americans

African Americans have lived in New York since its early years, when many were slaves. After the city abolished slavery in 1827, more moved there from the South, where slavery was still allowed. Even more made the journey north during World War II.
By the 1950s about one million black people lived in the area of Harlem, very often in poor slum housing. Since the 1970s the situation has improved, but many black New Yorkers have moved away to areas such as the Bronx.

African Americans form about 25 percent ▲ of the New York population and make a vital contribution to the life of the city.

NEW YORK

BUILDINGS AND BRIDGES

The most famous buildings in New York are the gleaming skyscrapers that soar high above the streets of Manhattan. The city also has 65 bridges that link the city's islands to the mainland and each other.

The Flatiron Building

The first real skyscraper in New York was the Flatiron Building at Fifth Avenue and 23rd Street. This steel-framed, stone-covered structure was completed in 1902 and is shaped like a long, narrow triangle. It was given its name because many people thought that it looked like an iron. Others think that it is more like the bow (front) of a ship. The building rises 285 feet (87 m) above the ground and has 21 stories.

▲ The strange shape of the Flatiron Building (left) makes the wind rush along the streets below. The spire of the Chrysler Building (right) is made of gleaming stainless steel.

◄ The Federal Hall National Memorial stands on the site where George Washington was sworn in as president. At the entrance is a statue of the great man.

The Chrysler Building

The Chrysler Building was built for Walter Chrysler, owner of the Chrysler motor car company. Architect William Van Alen designed this 77-story **Art Deco** masterpiece and used a car theme for many of its special features – for example, its eagle decorations are based on car bonnet mascots. When the 1,046-foot (319-m) skyscraper was finished in 1930, it was the world's tallest building.

Major World Cities

The Empire State Building

In 1931 the new, 1,250-foot (381-m) tall Empire State Building beat the Chrysler's height record. This 102-story skyscraper was built at the rate of over four stories each week. Sandwich stands were set up on several floors so that workers did not waste time going down to the street to buy food. In 1945 an American bomber flew into the building. Fourteen people were killed, but the skyscraper stayed upright.

The World Trade Center

In 1973 the 110-story World Trade Center took over from the Empire State as New York's highest building. One of its twin towers was 1,364 feet (416 m) tall, the other a yard shorter. in 1993, a terrorist bomb exploded in a car park underneath the building, killing six people, and in 2001 a terrorist attack destroyed both towers. A permanent memorial has been built on the site, now known as Ground Zero.

GRAND CENTRAL TERMINAL

Grand Central Terminal (below) is not only a busy railway station but also a stunning **Beaux-Arts** building. The huge stone and marble structure opened in 1913. Among its magnificent features are a sweeping staircase and a giant, sculpture-covered clock. The terminal was made a protected National Landmark in 1978 and has recently been restored to its original glory. The ceiling was cleaned so that the design of zodiac signs and 2,500 stars on a bright blue background can be clearly seen.

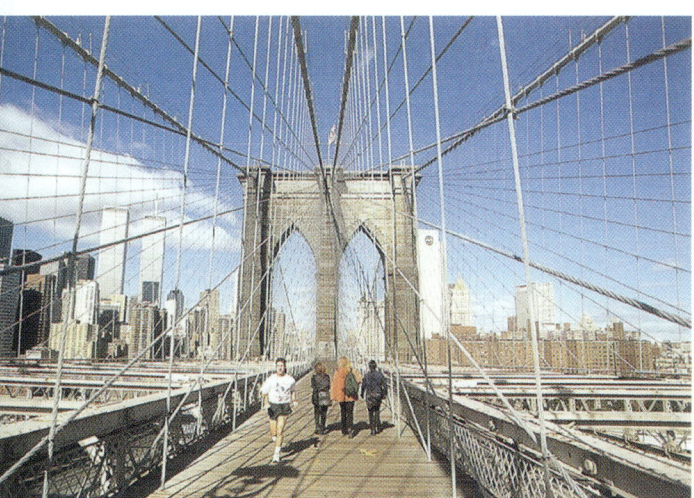

▲ People crossing Brooklyn Bridge. This picture also shows the World Trade Center (the two tall towers on the left) before its destruction.

Brooklyn Bridge

The 1,595-foot (486-m) Brooklyn Bridge spans the East River, linking Brooklyn and Manhattan. Its architect, John Roebling, died before construction began. His son, Washington, got the **bends** after working on the project under water and was paralysed. Accidents killed 20 builders and, after the bridge opened in 1883, 12 people died in a stampede. Now the tragic past is largely forgotten and the bridge is admired for its beauty.

OPEN SPACES

 Early city planners did not think that New York needed many parks. They believed that enough fresh air blew in from the sea to keep people healthy and happy. Yet now the city has over 49,000 acres of parkland.

Central Park

Until the mid-19th century much of central Manhattan was home to farming settlements and other small communities. Then newspaper editor William Cullen Bryant persuaded city leaders to turn the area into a park. Central Park, as it became known, was designed by Frederick Law Olmsted and Calvert Vaux. Now its 840 acres contain half a million trees, several lakes, a roller-skating rink, a theater, the Metropolitan Museum of Art, and much more.

▲ Many New Yorkers enjoy walking, jogging, cycling or rollerblading in Central Park.

▲ Castle Clinton now stands in Battery Park. The park is named after the **battery** of cannons that the castle once contained.

Hudson greenbelt

Another large green space in Manhattan was created during the 1980 and improved greatly in recent years. Battery Park is on the borough's southern tip. It was built on rubble dug up during construction of the World Trade Center. Since the mid-2010s, a wide and popular "greenbelt" of connected parks, promenades, bike paths, and walkways has been built. Strollers and riders can now walk along the waterfront from below the Manhattan Bridge all the way around the edge of Manhattan to the West 60s.

16   Major World Cities

Flushing Meadows-Corona Park

The borough of Queens contains the Flushing Meadows-Corona Park, which covers 1,230 acres. The park is best known as the home of the US Open Tennis Championships. It also contains the Unisphere, a giant steel ball that weighs over 330 tons and was originally built for a fair in 1964. The park houses a wildlife center, too, devoted to North American animals.

Daring acrobats entertain the crowds in Washington Square, at the heart of fashionable Greenwich Village.

Bronx Zoo

Bronx Zoo, the biggest in New York, is home to about 4,000 animals and 500 birds. Many are kept in open areas similar to their natural habitats. For example, rainforest creatures roam the Jungle World exhibit, while mountain animals, such as snow leopards, live in a mini-Himalayas. There is also a children's zoo, where young visitors can enjoy activities such as climbing up artificial spiders' webs.

New York Botanical Garden

Just north of the Bronx Zoo is the New York **Botanical Garden**. Its features include a huge glass conservatory with a crystal dome. Inside there are many exotic plants, such as palms, as well as a desert area. The city has several other botanical gardens, including one in Brooklyn which includes a collection of bonsai trees and a Japanese garden.

ON THE BEACH

There are beaches in many parts of New York. One of the most popular is Coney Island Beach in Brooklyn. Visitors there can swim in the sea, enjoy the amusement park (left), eat hot dogs and visit the New York Aquarium, which contains about 10,000 fish. Further afield is the Rockaways, a finger of land that juts out into the Atlantic Ocean. Here the waves are strong enough for surfing.

NEW YORK

HOMES AND HOUSING

The people of New York have always included both rich and poor. The wide variety of housing in the city reflects the huge differences in wealth of its inhabitants.

Tenements and projects

From about 1850, builders began to construct brick tenements as homes for immigrants in the Lower East Side. The apartments were cramped and unhygienic and **tuberculosis** quickly spread. Tenement designs were later improved, but the blocks are still slums, many of them lived in by Puerto Rican immigrants. Thousands of poor New Yorkers also live in **housing projects**.

▼ In 1867 the New York authorities passed a law requiring all tenement buildings to have fire escapes. These metal stairs still exist.

▲ During the 19th century, Little Italy was full of new immigrants. Large families lived in tiny apartments and people opened shops below.

Row houses

As poor immigrants moved into southern Manhattan, middle-class families moved north. Land was expensive, so many people bought or built row houses rather than wide, detached homes. Many row houses were brownstones, so called because they were made of red-brown sandstone. These homes, in areas such as Chelsea, are still very popular.

Millionaires' mansions

New York's richest 19th-century citizens did not have to worry about the cost of housing. They built mansions in fashionable areas such as Fifth Avenue, east of Central Park. This is still one of the city's most chic addresses, but there are now more apartments than mansions. There are also many expensive homes west of Central Park, especially along Riverside Drive.

18

Major World Cities

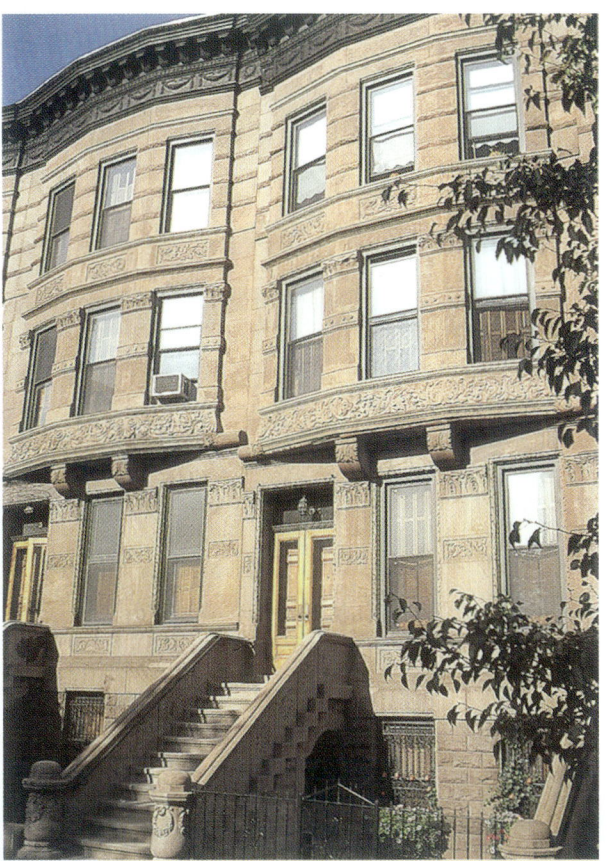

▲ Typical New York brownstones. Each house has a stoop—a small flight of steps outside that leads to a door platform.

SoHo and TriBeCa

SoHo, the district *S*outh of *Ho*uston Street in Manhattan, was once an industrial area. Now it is home to artists and others who moved in when housing in nearby Greenwich Village became too expensive. Since the 1960s many people have converted SoHo warehouses into **lofts**. Others have moved into the area's 19th-century houses with cast-iron fronts. Now SoHo is expensive, so people are moving to nearby TriBeCa, the *Tri*angle *Be*low *Ca*nal Street, and making new lofts there.

Battery Park City

Battery Park City lies next to Battery Park and was also built on rubble from the World Trade Center site. Builders have constructed several expensive apartment blocks, both low- and high-rise, in the area. Residents can enjoy many new facilities, including a walkway along the Hudson River lined with trees and ponds.

THE DAKOTA BUILDING

The Dakota apartment building stands on 72nd Street, just west of Central Park. When it opened in 1884 it was the first luxury housing in the area. Many famous people have lived there over the years. They include the pop star John Lennon, who was shot dead outside the building in 1980. Lennon's widow, Yoko Ono lives in the Dakota. She created the Strawberry Fields garden in Central Park, opposite the building, as a memorial to her husband.

▲ In the 19th and early 20th centuries Greenwich Village was a rich, quiet suburb. The beautiful homes of Grove Court are among many remaining from that era.

EDUCATION

The New York authorities encourage learning for people of all ages and run thousands of schools and colleges. The city also provides private education.

Public and private

Before the mid-19th century, many children in the USA received little or no education. Most of those who did go to school went to private, church or charity institutions. Then, in 1853, free, public education for all children began in New York City. Private education still exists, but it is far less common.

School system

American children must complete 12 years of education. In New York City this lasts from the ages of 6 to 17. Children begin at elementary school, move on to middle school, and finish at high school, where most gain a diploma. Many parents now start their children's schooling early by sending them to kindergarten.

▲ A typical New York City school playground. The wall next to the school has been decorated with brightly colored murals.

Local school boards

The New York Board of Education is in overall charge of public schooling in the city, but local school boards run its elementary and middle schools on a day-to-day basis. They have to deal with different conditions in different areas. In poor districts, they may have to work for better school buildings. In areas with many immigrants they may have to employ staff to teach pupils English.

◄ School buses like this take many New York children safely to their schools in the morning and home again in the evening.

20

Major World Cities

New York universities

New York has six main universities. The oldest, Columbia University in Manhattan, is private. It was founded in 1754 and belongs to the **Ivy League**. For many years, only men could study there, while women went to Barnard College nearby. Since 1983 the university has been for both men and women. New York University, in Greenwich Village, is the largest private university in the US, while the large City University of New York is publicly funded.

▲ The buildings of Columbia University are on the upper West Side. They include the domed Low Memorial Library (above).

THE SCHOMBURG CENTER

The Schomburg Center for Research in Black Culture lies in the center of Harlem. It contains the world's biggest collection of books, films, and other material about the history of black people in the US and their present-day ways of life. There are about five million items in all, some on display in the Center's museum, others in its library. The Center is used by scholars and other visitors who value this unique place to study.

Specialized education

New York offers a variety of high schools for pupils who want to specialize from their teenage years, for example the School of the Performing Arts. There are also many specialized higher education centers. Rockefeller University is the place for scientific and medical research. The Juilliard School in the Lincoln Center is where musicians, dancers, and actors learn their skills.

◀ The Juilliard School is named after Augustus D. Juilliard, who in the 1920s left money in his will to set it up.

NEW YORK

RELIGION

New York City is one of the most religiously diverse urban areas in the world, with every major religion heavily represented.

Early churches

Many of the first Europeans in New York were **Protestant** Christians. In 1654, when the city was still New Amsterdam, a Protestant church was built in Flatbush, Brooklyn. A later church now stands there, but old Dutch graves remain in the cemetery. Another early church was Trinity Church, which opened in Manhattan in 1846.

▲ A gospel choir made up of men, women, and children sings at a service in a church in Harlem.

Protestantism today

More than 15 percent of New Yorkers are **Baptists**. Many of these are African Americans who attend churches in Harlem, famous for their stirring **gospel** choirs. Many other Protestants belong to the **Episcopal Church**. Their biggest place of worship is the Cathedral of St. John the Divine. Construction of the church began in 1892 and will not end before 2050. When it does, the cathedral will be the world's largest.

Roman Catholicism

Roman Catholicism is the religion of more New Yorkers than any other—over 20 percent of the city's population are members. Many belong to families that originally came from Ireland or Italy, where Catholicism is the main faith. The most important Catholic church in New York, and the largest in the US, is St. Patrick's Cathedral on Fifth Avenue, Manhattan. It was completed in 1879.

22

Judaism

The first group of Jews to settle in New York—there were just 23—arrived from Brazil in 1654. The Jewish community grew slowly until the late 19th century, when immigration soared. Now about 11 percent of New Yorkers are Jewish. Some belong to the Orthodox branch of Judaism, others to a more liberal tradition. Major Jewish places of worship in the city are Temple Emanu-El on Fifth Avenue and the Eldridge Street Synagogue on the Lower East Side.

Islam

There are thousands of Muslims in New York. Some are native New Yorkers, others come from all around the world. The city contains many mosques (places of worship), including some for particular Islamic groups, for example the Turkish community. The most important mosque in the city is in Manhattan's Islamic Cultural Center. An Islamic school is now being built there too.

▲ All mosques must point towards Mecca, where Mohammed, the founder of Islam, was born. The correct position for New York's Islamic Cultural Center was worked out by computer.

◀ St. Patrick's Cathedral was designed by architect James Renwick. When it was built in the 19th century, it stood on the edge of New York City. Now it is in the center.

BUDDHA AND CONFUCIUS

Many members of New York's Chinese community are Buddhists. There are many Buddhist temples in Manhattan's Chinatown, including this one (left). Some Chinese people follow the teachings of Confucius. A bronze statue of this wise man, who lived in China from 551 to 479 BC. stands in Chinatown, on the edge of Confucius Plaza.

NEW YORK 23

INDUSTRY AND FINANCE

New York has many factories and banks, as well as tourist and media industries. It is the world center of some industries, especially finance centered on Wall Street.

Docks in decline

New York was once the USA's busiest port. By the 1890s huge amounts of American produce were being brought along railways, the Eric Canal and the Hudson River to its docks for transport abroad. Some cargo ships still sail in and out of the city, but more use ports in nearby New Jersey, which have more modern facilities.

▲ Huge sailing ships line the quayside at South Street in this busy scene from the 1870s.

The manufacturing industry

Thousands of 19th-century immigrants worked in New York's clothing factories, where conditions were often dangerous. In 1911 a fire at the Triangle Shirtwaist Factory killed 146 people, forcing the authorities to introduce safety laws. Clothing is still a big New York business, especially in Manhattan's Garment District. Another major industry is food-processing. But many companies have moved out of the city as rents and wages are so high.

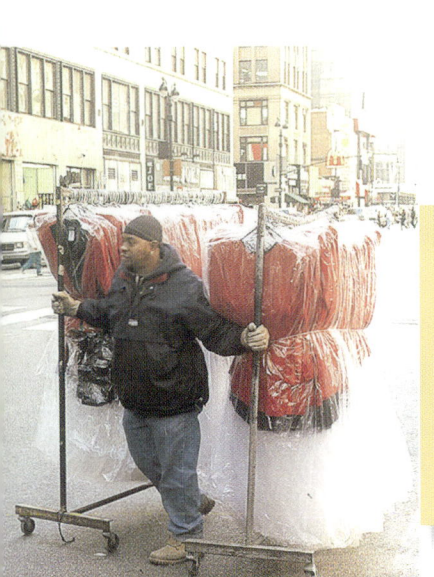

◄ A Garment District worker wheels a rack of new clothes from a factory to a nearby warehouse. About 200,000 people work in the Garment District.

TOURIST TRADE

About 56 million tourists visit New York each year, over 10 million of them from abroad. A wealthy few still sail in on luxury liners, but most arrive by air. The tourist trade provides work for thousands of New Yorkers, from tour guides showing people around the city, to work in restaurants, hotels, museums and theaters.

Major World Cities

The Financial District

New York's Financial District covers the southern tip of Manhattan. The New York Stock Exchange, on Wall Street, is at its heart. It was set up in 1792 and people have bought and sold shares there ever since. The Wall Street Crash of 1929 led to serious losses. One of the US government's main banks stands nearby. It contains more than 500,000 gold bars, so security is very tight.

Banks and businesses

There are many other banks and businesses in the Financial District. Some are in the World Finance Center, while others, such as the mighty Chase Manhattan Bank, have their own, specially designed headquarters. There are major companies in Midtown Manhattan, too, especially in the Rockefeller Center. But the many businesses once based in the World Trade Center have had to find alternative accommodation.

◀ There are 21 separate buildings in the giant Rockefeller Center. Towering over them all is the 850-foot-high Comcast Building, containing the offices of many different companies.

Media world

Book, newspaper and magazine publishing is an important New York industry. Much of this is based in Midtown Manhattan. Newspapers include *The New York Times* and *The Wall Street Journal*. Many TV and radio stations have bases in the city. They include the National Broadcasting Company (NBC), which has studios in the Rockefeller Center. Top advertising agencies can be found on Madison Avenue.

The Wall Street Journal is essential reading ▶ for people who want to follow the rise and fall of their shares as well as the latest news.

NEW YORK

CRIME AND PUNISHMENT

New York was once famous for its high levels of crime, including murder. Things have been improving since the early 1990s under a series of law-and-order mayors, but the city still has problems.

The NYPD

The New York Police Department (NYPD) fights crime across the city. New York has 76 police districts, each with its own commander, officers and station. The city's Police Headquarters is on Police Plaza, near City Hall. NYPD officers wear blue trousers, shirts and ties and a peaked cap with a gold badge. All are armed with guns. Unofficial law enforcers called Guardian Angels try to assist the police by patrolling streets and subways.

▲ William Marcy 'Boss' Tweed was a 19th-century leader of the New York Democratic Party. He took bribes and stole city funds worth $200 million, but was later imprisoned and died in jail.

▲ Both men and women serve in the NYPD. The force's badge appears on their shirt sleeves and on the official cars they drive.

Cracking crime

The police work to beat crime in many ways. For example, Street Crimes Units patrol dangerous areas such as the Bronx. Details of crimes are fed into computers then analysed to work out when and where criminals are likely to strike again. Since the introduction of these and other tactics, crimes have decreased.

Major World Cities

PROHIBITION

In 1920 the US government banned the manufacture and sale of alcohol and the **Prohibition** era began. Thousands of people in New York, as elsewhere in the country, did not obey the new laws. Criminals called **bootleggers** produced and sold alcohol illegally. Other people set up clubs called speakeasies where customers bought alcohol (right). During the depression that followed the Wall Street Crash, the government needed to find jobs for people wherever it could, even in alcohol manufacturing. So, in 1933, it abolished Prohibition.

City crimes

Even with improvements, some crimes still occur regularly in New York. Among them are pickpocketing, assault, and car theft. Illegal drug use is also common. Racial violence sometimes flares up, too, for example between the black and Jewish communities in Crown Heights, Brooklyn in the 1990s or against Muslim communities following the World Trade Center attacks.

High-profile crimes

In 2014, an African American man died after being arrested, sparking outrage and civil unrest. In late 2014, New York City police men were targeted by gunmen reacting to events in other cities; two NYPD cops were killed in their car. Major nonviolent crimes have occurred at Wall Street banks and brokerage houses.

▲ New York police stand at attention during the funeral of Officer Rafael Ramos, one of two officers shot while sitting in their car.

Going to Court

There are many courts in New York City. Some try people for crimes against federal (national) laws, others for crimes against state laws. Several of them—including the US Courthouse and the Criminal Courts Building—stand in Manhattan's Civic Center.

NEW YORK

GETTING AROUND

New Yorkers seem to be always on the move. In Manhattan the pavement is full of scurrying pedestrians, while cars, buses and taxis jam the roads. Subway trains are packed and even harbors are busy as ferries sail in and out.

▲ Yellow taxis and private cars move bumper to bumper along the six lanes of Manhattan's busy 42nd Street.

On the road

Driving in central New York is only for the daring, so people often take one of the famous yellow taxis instead. There are about 13,500 of them in the city. Many are driven by new immigrants. The rise of smartphone-driven Uber cars has threatened the popularity of taxis. Another way to get around overground is to take a bus. Two hundred routes cross the city, but buses, like cars, are often stuck in traffic. Long-distance buses run from the Port Authority Bus Terminal.

Subway system

New York's first subway (underground) line opened in 1904. Now the system has 469 stations and is used by over five million people every day. There are two types of subway train. Local trains stop at every station. Express trains go faster and miss out some stations. The subway was once dirty and dangerous. A citywide cleanup campaign and new equipment has made the subway system much improved.

◄ New York's express buses do not make many stops, so they go much faster than regular buses—but they still cannot avoid the jams.

28 Major World Cities

Rail travel

Manhattan has four main railway stations. Trains run on an amazing 123 lines in and out of Grand Central Terminal. Local trains to New Jersey use the stations on Sixth Avenue and at the World Trade Center. Penn (Pennsylvania) Station is a terminus for both commuter services and long-distance trains.

▲ A train waits at a Grand Central Terminal platform. Most trains from this station carry workers in and out of New York every day.

FULL STEAM AHEAD

In 1807 American engineer Robert Fulton launched the *Clermont*, a **paddle-wheel steamboat**, in New York City. It made its way up the Hudson River to Albany in just 32 hours—three times faster than sailing boats. Soon this fast method of transport was being used to carry goods from inland and western areas to New York. This was one reason why the city became a major port.

On the water

New York can easily be explored by water. Regular ferries take passengers from Battery Park to the Statue of Liberty, providing them with superb views of Manhattan. The ferries also visit Ellis Island. Longer cruises are available on boats and catamarans. The Passenger Ship Terminal on the West Side receives cruise lines from around the world.

Air travel

New York has three major airports. The main international airport is John F. Kennedy (JFK), in the borough of Queens. Flights to and from other parts of the US fly in and out of La Guardia Airport, also in Queens. Newark Airport in New Jersey is used for international and internal travel. Helicopter sightseeing trips fly from three Manhattan heliports.

▲ The Staten Island Ferry, which travels from Manhattan to Staten Island, is free and operates 24 hours a day. It is used by tourists and working New Yorkers alike.

SHOPS AND MARKETS

New York City, especially Manhattan, is a shopper's paradise. But buyers must beware—after a day's serious spending, their bags will be full but their wallets will be empty and their feet sore.

Department stores

There are dozens of department stores in New York. Among them is Macy's, the world's largest. It opened on Broadway in 1858, where it still stands. Clothes, cosmetics and other goods are sold on its ten floors. The famous Bloomingdale's store sells a wide range of goods, including clothing and gourmet foods. Saks Fifth Avenue is a high-end store featuring men's and women's clothing.

Fine fashions

Many New York stores specialize in clothes. Designers such as Christian Dior have shops on and around Fifth and Madison Avenues. SoHo is the place to buy more unusual outfits. The city also has many vintage clothing stores, including Pilgrim New York on the Lower East Side, with a wide range of offerings.

▲ Thousands of people flood through the doors of Macy's department store every day. If they grow tired of shopping, they can eat there, too.

Diamond-dealing

People looking for jewelry to go with their high-fashion clothes are spoiled for choice in New York. They can head for specialist stores such as Cartier and Tiffany's on Fifth Avenue. Or they can go to Manhattan's Diamond District and deal directly with gem, gold, and silver traders, as well as independent jewelers. Experts are also on hand to string their precious purchases to make unique necklaces and bracelets.

◀ Chic clothes in the windows of Bergdorf Goodman's Fifth Avenue store are designed to attract wealthy shoppers.

Children's choice

Children can find plenty of places to spend their money in New York, but they'll have the best luck on Times Square. Several major kid-related stores anchor the massive revival of the venerable area. Toys R Us, the Disney Store, and the nearby Lego Store are joined by brand-name outlets for M&Ms and Hershey's candy. Nintendo World appeals to video gamers, while SoHo's Forbidden Planet is one-stop shopping for comic and fantasy fans.

▲ A jewelry store in 47th Street, known as Diamond Row. Many of the traders are Jews who had to leave their diamond businesses in Holland before World War II.

▲ This New York florist has created a spectacular autumn display, mixing vibrant orange pumpkins with bright red and yellow flowers.

NEW YORK MARKETS

There are many types of market in New York. The Annex on Sixth Avenue is one of the best **flea markets**. It is held at weekends and items for sale on its 600 stalls include antiques. **Greenmarkets** are very popular. One of the biggest takes place on Union Square, where farmers sell fresh produce and home-cooked foods such as herbs, honey and **pretzels**. Manhattan's main flower market is on Sixth Avenue, but not all the plants on show are for sale to the public. Many are bought by professional florists, who use them to decorate grand homes and offices.

Book-buying

Adults and children alike can enjoy browsing in New York's 500-plus book shops. Barnes & Noble stores are all around the city and provide people with sofas to sit on while they make their choice. Antiquarian book stores such as Argosy are treats for history fans. Strand Book Store on Broadway is the largest second-hand book shop in the USA. It stocks about two million different titles.

FOOD AND DRINK

New Yorkers love their food, and the city's 19,000 restaurants offer a banquet of choices. Thanks to the many immigrant communities, there is a huge variety of cooking. Everything from Jewish **bagels** to Japanese **sushi** can be found here.

Eating out

Hard-working New Yorkers are always in a hurry and many people eat out more often than at home. The day might start with breakfast at a diner. This might he eggs sunny side up with bacon, waffles, or syrup-drenched pancakes, juice, and coffee, or just a Danish pastry with coffee. Lunch might be a **deli** sandwich or some other fast food. At dinner the serious eating begins.

American dishes

Food from all over the Americas is available in New York. One of the most famous restaurants serving traditional North American dishes, such as meatloaf, is the Empire Diner in Chelsea. Sylvia's in Harlem offers food from the American South, such as fried chicken. During the mid-morning Gospel Brunch, a choir sings while customers eat.

▲This fish shop in Chinatown sells all kinds of fresh seafood. Many of the items here are sold to local restaurants.

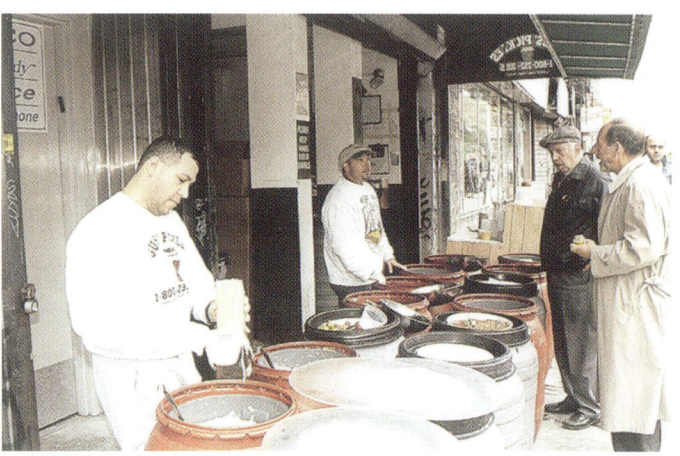

TOP FOOD SHOPS

New York has many fine food stores. Two of the most famous are on Broadway—Zabar's, known for its Jewish delicacies such as lox (smoked salmon), and Dean & DeLuca which features Italian and other specialities. Balducci's food store, in Greenwich Village, grew from a street stall to a huge shop. Street food stalls are also popular, such as this one selling Jewish-style pickles (left).

32   **Major World Cities**

Ethnic cooking

Jewish food is extremely popular in New York. It can be enjoyed at places such as Yonah Schimmel's, which specializes in bagels and stuffed pastries called *knishes*. Italian cooking is also a favorite. There are many Italian restaurants in Little Italy and John's in Greenwich Village makes some of the best pizzas in the city. A huge variety of Chinese food is available in Chinatown, from steamed dumplings to crispy duck.

▼ Great steak restaurants have long been part of the New York restaurant scene. Smith & Wollensky on Third Avenue has become a national chain.

Expensive eating

New York also offers ultra-expensive restaurants, some more famous for their customers than their cooking. Top spots include the Four Seasons, where paintings by Picasso decorate the walls, and Lutece, where diners eat by a large fountain. The Peter Luger restaurant on Broadway specializes in steak, as it has done since it opened in 1887.

Fast food

New York contains every kind of traditional fast food outlet, from hamburger restaurants to hot dog stands. But there is more on offer, too. Delis will make almost any kind of sandwich—a New York favorite is pastrami (smoked, spiced beef) on rye bread. Cafés serve drinks, snacks, and cakes, including cheesecake, a specialty of the city.

◀ Sausages, hot dogs, *knishes*, pretzels, and soft drinks are all for sale at this New York fast food stall.

NEW YORK 33

ENTERTAINMENT

The New York entertainment scene is among the best in the world, offering everything from serious theater and opera to popular films and baseball games.

Broadway and beyond

The area around Times Square is the center of New York's Theater District. It is known as Broadway, but also includes other streets nearby. There are about 40 Broadway theaters, which stage popular musicals and comedies. Serious works are often produced at smaller **Off-Broadway** venues such as the Joseph Papp Public Theater. It is owned by the city authorities and runs an annual Shakespeare Festival. Even smaller, Off-Off-Broadway theaters also put on shows.

▲ Radio City Music Hall stands near Rockefeller Center. Since the 1930s many famous stars have performed there.

Movie mania

Many big New York movie theaters are in the Times Square district. There are also multi-screen venues elsewhere, such as in the Village or on the Upper East Side. Some movie theaters specialize in classic American films or films from abroad. New York's main Imax cinema is part of a Broadway multiplex.

▼ Dancers from the Alvin Ailey American Dance Theater performing at City Center, a popular modern dance venue.

Classical music

One of the main venues for classical music is Lincoln Center on the Upper West Side. Buildings that make up the Center include the Metropolitan Opera House, the New York State Theater, where the New York Opera and New York Ballet perform, and the Avery Fisher Hall, home of the New York Philharmonic Orchestra.

Major World Cities

Jazz and rock

New York caters to fans of many other types of music, too. Jazz lovers can take their pick from several top clubs in the city. Among the most famous are the Village Vanguard, which dates from 1935, and the Blue Note. Both are in Greenwich Village. Major rock stadiums include Madison Square Garden, which can house an audience of about 20,000.

Sports scene

New Yorkers love to participate in sport, if only by jogging around Central Park. They also support their professional teams. The city's most successful baseball team is the New York Yankees, who play at Yankee Stadium in the Bronx. The New York Mets, whose home is Citi Field in Queens, have many followers, too. The New York Knicks play pro basketball while the New York Rangers play pro hockey, both at Madison Square Garden, also a venue for major boxing contests.

THE HARLEM RENAISSANCE

An important black cultural movement emerged in Harlem in the 1920s. Poets such as Langston Hughes, novelists such as Zora Neale Hurston, and artists such as Archibald Motley were all part of it. But now people are more likely to remember the entertainers, such as jazz pianist and composer Duke Ellington and band leader Cab Calloway. Both played at the famous Cotton Club (above). Jazz singer Billie Holiday also began her career in the clubs of Harlem.

◀ The new Yankee Stadium opened in 2009 as one of baseball's largest venues. It replaced an older stadium that had stood in the Bronx since 1923.

MUSEUMS AND GALLERIES

There are over 150 museums in New York, including several that contain major art collections. The city also has about 500 private galleries, showing a wide variety of works.

▲ The Met contains more than 300 exhibition rooms, some of which house temporary displays. Banners outside announce these shows.

Metropolitan Museum of Art

The 250-room Metropolitan Museum of Art (the Met) contains over three million objects. These include paintings by many of the world's finest artists, including Rembrandt and Van Gogh, as well as precious ancient objects from around the world. The Met also contains a complete building, the Ancient Egyptian Temple of Dendur.

MOMA

The Museum of Modern Art (MOMA) has a stunning collection, but none of its 150,000 treasures dates from before 1880. The museum contains works by artists such as Monet, Picasso, and New Yorker Andy Warhol. One of Warhol's famous pictures of Marilyn Monroe hangs here. The museum also displays photographs, sculpture and more.

The Guggenheim Museum

The huge white whorl of the Guggenheim Museum (1959) was designed by American architect Frank Lloyd Wright, and is itself worth a close look. The museum was built to hold the art collection of its rich founder, Solomon R Guggenheim. It contains works by famous modern artists such as Paul Klee and Vasili Kandinsky.

▲ The Guggenheim Museum's spiral shape has earned it the nickname "The Big Seashell." There is another, smaller, Guggenheim in the SoHo area.

Major World Cities

South Street Seaport

The Seaport was New York's long-ago home of major shipping and cargo lines, and then a fish market. It became a popular tourist spot when a mall was built on Pier 17. However, a 2011 storm surge caused by Hurricane Sandy caused great damage to the once-vibrant area. It is in the process of being rebuilt. Visitors can still go onboard several ships that remain on exhibit.

▲ Visitors onboard the Intrepid can tour the massive ship's below-decks area as well as see aircraft and the Space Shuttle *Enterprise*.

The American Museum of Natural History

Packed with 36 million items, this is the largest natural history museum in the world and probably the largest museum of any kind. The dinosaur display has some of the most exciting exhibits, but there is much more to see, including a 95-foot-long blue whale and the Star of India, the biggest blue sapphire ever found. The museum also has a **planetarium**.

The Intrepid Sea-Air-Space Museum

Floating on the Hudson River, alongside Pier 86, is an old US Navy aircraft carrier called the *Intrepid*. Visitors can climb aboard to view jet fighters, spy planes and many other exhibits that tell the story of warfare at sea and in the air, as well as the history of sea and space exploration. There is also a submarine next to the ship that people can look inside.

ELLIS ISLAND

From 1892 all immigrants who arrived in New York had to disembark at Ellis Island, where they were registered and examined by doctors. They also had to answer questions about their political beliefs. More than 12 million people had passed through the island by 1954, when it was abandoned. In 1990 its buildings were re-opened as an Immigration Museum (left). Visitors follow the path immigrants took and hear recordings of their moving stories.

SPECIAL EVENTS

New Yorkers never have a reason to be bored. There is something to do all year round, from the depths of winter to the height of summer.

Warming up

There are several ways for people to take their minds off the freezing temperatures of January and February. They can head to Chinatown to watch, or join in, celebrations for Chinese New Year. The festivities include dragon dances and exploding firecrackers. In February, any New Yorkers with enough stamina can do the Empire State Building Run-Up. Climbing the 1,860 steps in a few minutes keeps out the cold.

▲ Young Irish dancers in traditional embroidered costumes take part in the lively St. Patrick's Day Parade.

Spring parades

The big event of early spring is the St. Patrick's Day Parade on the weekend nearest to March 17. St. Patrick is the **patron saint** of Ireland and the Irish community celebrates in style. Thousands of people march through the city and bands play rousing Irish music. At Easter there is a parade from Central Park to the Rockefeller Center, in which women traditionally wear flowery bonnets.

▲ Spectacular fireworks explode high above New York during Independence Day festivities.

Sporting season

As the weather improves, the number of sporting events grows. The baseball season begins in April and in May the Great Five Borough Bike Tour takes place. Thousands of people complete the 42-mile (68-m) course. May 17 is Martin Luther King Memorial Day, when a parade commemorates the work of this great activist for black **civil rights**.

38

Major World Cities

Summer highlight

The highlight of summer is the celebration on July 4, Independence Day. This marks the date in 1776 when the US declared its independence from Great Britain. The Stars and Stripes **Regatta** is held at South Street Seaport, Macy's department store sponsors a fireworks display and the New York Philharmonic Orchestra plays in Central Park.

Autumn arrivals

In September both the US Open Tennis Championships and the New York Film Festival take place, the film festival continuing into October. On October 12, the Columbus Day Parade marks the 1492 arrival in the Americas of explorer Christopher Columbus. The New York Marathon is run in November, from Staten Island all the way to Central Park.

▲ The massive main stadium at the US Open is named for Arthur Ashe, the first African American to win a major men's tennis tournament.

THANKSGIVING

Thanksgiving, on the fourth Thursday in November, is a time of great celebration. It marks the day in 1621 when the **Pilgrims** celebrated their first harvest in Massachusetts. In New York, Macy's store organizes a Thanksgiving Day Parade down Broadway. There are floats and bands and massive, helium-filled balloons in the shape of cartoon characters.

Christmas and Chanukah

At Christmas New York's streets are decorated and a huge tree is put up at the Metropolitan Museum of Art. The Jewish festival of Chanukah takes place at about the same time. A giant menorah (an eight-branched candlestick) stands on Fifth Avenue for its eight days. On December 31, more than a million poeple gather in Times Square for New Year's Eve.

◀ The world watches as New Yorkers celebrate New Year's Eve in Times Square. A light-covered crystal ball drops at midnight to cheers.

CITY CHARACTERS

Over the years people with many skills have worked to make New York such a vibrant metropolis. Here are just a few of them.

Frederick Law Olmsted

American landscape designer Frederick Law Olmsted became superintendent of the future Central Park in 1857. The next year, with architect Calvert Vaux, he began work on his plan to create the park. He wanted it to be for the poor as well as the rich and to contain woods and lakes. He later designed other New York parks, such as Prospect Park in Brooklyn.

◂ Frederick Law Olmsted's aim in creating Central Park was to bring the countryside to the city. Many people think he succeeded.

Andrew Carnegie

Scotsman Andrew Carnegie arrived in the USA as a boy in 1848. He became a millionaire by working and investing in railways, oil, and steel, then used his fortune to do good works—for example he made a donation of $125 million to set up the Carnegie Corporation of New York in 1911. Funds from this organization were used to improve the city. Some of the money paid for Carnegie Hall, still a major concert venue.

◂ Andrew Carnegie's first job was in a cotton mill, where he earned $1.20 a week. By 1905 he was rich enough to own the huge mansion in this picture.

Major World Cities

Dorothy Parker

Dorothy Parker was born in New Jersey in 1893 but was educated in New York City. She became first a critic, working for magazines such as *The New Yorker*, then a poet and short-story writer. Dorothy Parker is remembered especially for her sharp wit. This was often on display at the Algonquin Round Table, a writers' group that met in New York's Algonquin Hotel during the 1920s and '30s.

▲ Dorothy Parker's work is still popular today. Many people visit the Algonquin Hotel on 44th Street to see where she and her friends met.

Woody Allen

Many people who have never visited New York have formed their idea of the city from the films of Woody Allen. Allen was born in Brooklyn in 1935. He made his first film in 1966 and rose to fame by writing, directing and starring in movies such as *Manhattan* (1979). He portrays New Yorkers, especially himself, as always worried about their lives and health. He now lives in the Upper East Side and is a keen supporter of the New York Knicks.

▲ One of Woody Allen's many talents is playing the clarinet. He often plays at Michael's Pub, a jazz club in central Manhattan.

Rudolph Giuliani

Italian-American Rudolph (Rudy) Giuliani was born in Brooklyn in 1944. He studied at New York University Law School, then worked his way up to become US **Attorney** for the Southern District of New York in 1983. In 1993 he was elected **Republican** mayor of New York City and in 1997 won a second term. Giuliani guided New Yorkers through the grim aftermath of the 2001 terrorist attack with calm determination and a strong spirit.

▲ Rudolph Giuliani's first swearing-in ceremony as mayor of New York took place in January 1994. His family watched as he took the oath.

THE FUTURE OF NEW YORK

Few American cities have faced a challenge as great as the one that New York City dealt with in the aftermath of the September 11, 2001, attacks. But in the decade-plus since, the city has truly been revitalized.

▲ Theaters, shopping, huge billboards, ticket agencies, restaurants, and more have turned Times Square into a world tourist mecca.

Cleaning up the city

The Times Square area, which was once very sleazy, is now the city's tourist centerpiece. Under former Mayor Michael Bloomberg, the city invested in new roadways and buildings. Major chain stores moved in, and theaters rebounded with packed houses. What was once a dirty, dangerous place has become a world showplace. Herald Square to the south has also improved, while many parts of Broadway have been turned into walkways and cafes.

Past and future

The events of September 11, 2001, will never be forgotten. A large museum and monument opened at "Ground Zero" in 2014 to honor the people who died in the attack. Also in 2014, the One World Trade Center building opened on the site of the fallen Twin Towers. It now dominates the Manhattan skyline and offers amazing views from its observation floors.

At 1,776 feet (541 m), One World Trade Center is the tallest building in the Western Hemisphere. ▶

Improving all over

The Bronx, with its high crime and poor housing, was for many years one of New York's biggest problems, but the "Bronx Miracle" revitalization has turned blighted areas into nicer ones. Brooklyn has become the "hot" place for young people to live, including many families. The arrival of new immigrant populations in Queens has greatly changed that borough. New construction on Staten Island has opened up new places for residence.

BLOOMING AREAS

Every few years, a different area of New York becomes fashionable. Nolita (*North* of *Little Italy*), NoHo (*North* of *Houston*), Park Slope (in Brooklyn), and Dumbo (Down Below the Manhattan Bridge) are some of the areas that are blooming with new residents.

◀ Site workers cleared about 1.5 million tons of debris from Ground Zero. On May 30, 2002 the recovery process was ended and a ceremony held for the workers and the victim's families.

Change ahead

On November 6, 2001, a new mayor was elected, Michael Bloomberg, a republican media tycoon. He made many changes to the city, including adding parks and making laws against smoking. In 2013, a much more liberal mayor named Bill di Blasio took over. He is expanding the social system in New York and has plans to provide more aid to poorer residents.

▲ Bill de Blasio and his wife Chirlane McCray have become a power couple in the city

NEW YORK

TIMELINE

This timeline shows some of the most important dates in the history of New York. All the events are mentioned earlier in the book.

PRE-16TH CENTURY

Native Americans of the **Algonquian** and **Iroquois** families inhabit the New York area

16TH CENTURY

1524
Italian explorer Giovanni da Verrazzano becomes first European to see future site of New York

17TH CENTURY

1609
Henry Hudson lands on Manhattan Island and sails down the future Hudson River
1624
Dutch West India Company sets up the **colony** of New Netherlands in the New York area
1625
First Dutch families move to Manhattan Island and found the town of New Amsterdam
1626
Peter Minuit becomes governor of New Amsterdam and buys it from Native Americans
1646
Peter Stuyvesant becomes governor of New Amsterdam
1653
Stuyvesant makes New Amsterdam a city
1664
British seize New Amsterdam and rename it New York

18TH CENTURY

1754
Columbia University founded
1775-83
The American Revolution; the British lose their American colonies, including New York, and the USA is founded
1789
New York becomes capital of the USA and **George Washington** is sworn in as the country's first president there
1790
Philadelphia replaces New York as US capital
1792
New York Stock Exchange established

19TH CENTURY

1800
New York population reaches 79,000
1811
Grid map for New York produced by the city commissioners
1820s
Mass immigration into New York begins
1825
Erie Canal opens
1827
Slavery abolished in New York
1842
Croton **Aqueduct** brings pure water to New York for the first time
1846
Trinity Church opens in Manhattan

1853
Free, public education for all begins in city
1858
Central Park laid out
1861-65
American Civil War leads to fighting and riots in New York
1879
St. Patrick's Cathedral completed
1883
Brooklyn Bridge opens
1884
Dakota Building completed
1886
Statue of Liberty unveiled
1892
Construction of Cathedral of St John the Divine begins
Ellis Island opens to receive immigrants
1898
Manhattan Island joins Queens, Brooklyn, Staten Island and the Bronx to form Greater New York, the modern city

20TH CENTURY

1902
Flatiron Building completed
1904
First New York subway opens
1911
146 people die in a fire at the Triangle Shirtwaist Factory
1913
Grand Central Terminal opens
1920s
Era of the Harlem Renaissance
1920-33
Prohibition era; alcohol banned
1929
The Wall Street Crash leads to economic depression

1930
Chrysler Building completed
1931
Empire State Building completed
1954
Ellis Island closes as immigrant center
1959
Guggenheim Museum opens
1973
World Trade Center opens
1975
New York is declared bankrupt
1987
Another Wall Street Crash
1990
Ellis Island reopens as a museum

21ST CENTURY

2000
Democrat Hillary Rodham Clinton elected US Senator for New York State
2001
Terrorist attack destroys World Trade Center and leaves more than 2,800 people dead
2009
Passenger airline crash lands in the Hudson River. Pilot gets plane to float long enough to rescue all passengers with help from local boats
2009
New York Yankees win 27th World Series title, extending their all-time lead
2011
"Occupy Wall Street" protesters gain world headlines calling for financial reform
2014
National September 11 Museum opens at Ground Zero, honoring those who lost their lives in 1993 and 2001 attacks
2014
One World Trade Center opens, becomes tallest building in Western Hemisphere

NEW YORK

GLOSSARY

Algonquian Of or belonging to a group of Native American peoples, for example the Wappinger, whose members speak languages of the Algonquian family.

aqueduct A large pipe for carrying water over a long distance.

Art Deco A style of art and architecture that was popular during the 1920s and '30s. It featured strong geometrical and sometimes also symmetrical shapes.

attorney A lawyer who is allowed to represent clients in court and at other legal proceedings.

bagels Chewy ring-shaped rolls that are boiled and baked.

Baptists Members of a Protestant Christian group that believes in baptizing people when they understand and accept the Christian faith, rather than as babies.

Beaux-Arts In the decorative style used in the Paris School of Fine Arts (Ecole des Beaux-Arts) in France.

bends Serious breathing difficulties, muscle pains and other problems caused by a sudden lowering of air pressure around the body. It often occurs in divers who return to the surface too quickly.

bootlegger A criminal who made and sold alcohol during Prohibition. Bootleggers were so called because former smugglers of illegal alcohol hid the bottles in their boot-tops.

botanical garden A garden where plants are studied by scientists as well as grown for public enjoyment.

Buddhist A member of a religion that began in India in about 500 BC. It is based on the teaching of a prince called Gautama Siddhartha. He was later given the title "Buddha," which means "enlightened one."

civil rights The rights of an individual, such as the right to freedom of speech, regardless of race or color.

civil war A war between different groups within a country rather than between separate countries.

colony A country that is occupied and ruled by the people of another country.

deli A shop where speciality foods and sandwiches are sold. The word is short for delicatessen.

Democrat A member of the Democratic Party, one of the two main political parties in the US. Democrats generally have more liberal views than Republicans.

depression A time of low business growth, high unemployment, and hardship.

Episcopal Church A branch of the Anglican Church, which also includes the Church of England.

flea market A market that sells a wide variety of low-priced, and sometimes second-hand, goods.

gospel A type of Christian religious music that was first sung by black people in the southern US.

Great Lakes Five lakes on or near the border between the US and Canada. They are: Superior, Huron, Erie, Ontario, and Michigan.

greenmarket A market to which country farmers bring meat, eggs, fruit, vegetables, and other produce for sale.

Hasidic Jews Members of a branch of Judaism (the Jewish religion) that began in 18th-century Poland. Hasidic men wear dark suits and hats.

housing projects Publicly funded housing developments designed for people who can afford only low rents.

immigrant A person who comes to live in a country where he or she was not born and is not a citizen.

Iroquois Of or belonging to a group of Native American peoples, such as the Mohawk, whose members speak languages of the Iroquoian family.

Ivy League The eight most highly regarded universities in the USA. They include Harvard, Yale and Columbia.

knishes Pastries stuffed with a filling such as potato or cheese.

kosher (of food) prepared according to Jewish religious laws.

Latinos US citizens whose ancestors came from Spanish-speaking parts of South and Central America.

lofts Spacious, usually high-ceilinged apartments located in a converted factory or warehouse.

longhouses Houses of the type built by some Native American peoples. They were long and narrow with rounded roofs and were made of wooden poles covered with sheets of bark.

Off-Broadway Of or relating to theaters that contain between 100 and 500 seats.

Orthodox Of or relating to the branch of Judaism that strictly follows ancient beliefs and teachings.

paddle-wheel steamboat A steam-driven boat with large wheels made of paddles (blades). The paddles are turned by the engine, making the boat move forward.

patron saint A saint who is believed to protect and care for a particular place, organization, or person.

Pilgrims The group of English Puritans (strict Protestants) who arrived in Massachusetts in 1620. They are also known as the Pilgrim Fathers.

planetarium A building where images of the stars and planets are projected on to a dark ceiling.

pretzels Hard, salty biscuits, often in the shape of knots.

Prohibition The era (1920-1933) during which selling or making alcohol was prohibited, or banned, in the US.

Protestant Of any Christian group that does not accept the authority of the Roman Catholic Church, but looks to the Bible as the source of religious truth.

regatta A series of yacht and other boat races.

Republican A member of the Republican Party, one of the two main political parties in the US. Republicans generally have more conservative views than Democrats.

Senator An elected member of the Senate, part of the US Congress. Each state elects two Senators.

shantytowns Groups of poorly built shacks or shelters.

sushi A Japanese dish of raw fish on top of cooked rice, shaped into small parcels.

Tammany Society The 19th-century New York Democratic Party that was based in Tammany Hall.

tenements Large housing blocks divided into apartments.

tuberculosis A serious, infectious disease that causes fever and often inflammation of the lungs.

United Nations An international organization formed in 1945, after World War II. It aims to promote world peace and to prevent further wars.

Wall Street Crash A financial crisis that took place in the US in 1929 and led to job losses and bankruptcies.

Washington, George (1732-1799) A politician and general who was commander in chief of America's armies during the American Revolution (1775-83). He was then the first president of the USA (1789-1797).

World War II A major war that lasted from 1939 to 1945 and involved a large number of countries. The Americans joined the war in 1941, fighting alongside the British, French, Russians, and others to defeat Germany and its allies.

INDEX

African Americans 5
Algonquian Native Americans 8, 44, 46
Allen, Woody 33, 41
American Museum of Natural History 6, 7, 37, 42
American Revolution 9, 44

banks 25
Battery Park 6, 7, 16, 19, 29
Battery Park City 19, 42
beaches 17
Belmont 12
Bernstein, Leonard 13
Bloomberg, Michael 43, 45
Bloomingdale's 30
Botanical Garden 17, 46
Broadway 4, 7, 30, 31, 32, 33, 34
Bronx, the 4, 6, 11, 12, 13, 17, 26, 43, 45
Bronx Zoo 17
Brooklyn 4, 6, 11, 12, 15, 17, 22, 40, 41, 45
Brooklyn Bridge 6, 7, 15, 45
Bryant, William Cullen 16
Buddhists 13, 22, 23, 46

Carnegie, Andrew 40
Castle Clinton 16
Cathedral of St John the Divine 6, 7, 22, 45
Central Park 6, 7, 10, 16, 18, 19, 38, 39, 40, 45
Chelsea 6, 7, 18, 32
Chinatown 6, 7, 12, 13, 23, 27, 32, 33, 38
Chrysler Building 6, 7, 14, 15, 45
City Hall 4, 5, 6, 7, 26
Civic Center 27
Civil War 11, 45, 46
Columbus, Christopher 39
Coney Island Beach 12, 17
Confucius Plaza 23
Cotton Club 35
Criminal Courts Building 27
Croton Aqueduct 10, 44, 46
Crown Heights 12, 27

Dakota Building 6, 7, 19, 45
di Blasio, Bill 43
Dutch West India Company 8, 9, 44

East River 4, 5, 15, 37
El Barrio (Spanish Harlem) 6, 7, 13
Eldridge Street Synagogue 23
Ellis Island 6, 7, 10, 16, 29, 37, 45
Empire State Building 6, 7, 15, 27, 38, 45
Eric Canal 10, 24, 44

Federal Hall National Memorial 14
Fifth Avenue 6, 7, 14, 18, 22, 23, 30, 31, 39
Financial District 6, 7, 9, 25
Flatiron Building 6, 7, 14, 45
Flushing Meadows-Corona Park 17

Garment District 6, 7, 24
Giuliani, Rudolph 26, 41, 43, 45
gospel choirs 22, 32, 46
Gracie Mansion 5, 6, 7
Grand Central Terminal 6, 7, 15, 29, 33, 45
Greenwich Village 6, 7, 17, 19, 21, 35
grid system 4, 10, 44
Ground Zero 6, 42, 43
Guggenheim Museum 6, 7, 36, 45

Harlem 6, 7, 11, 13, 18, 21, 22, 32, 35, 43, 45
Hell's Kitchen 6, 7, 12
Hudson, Henry S. 44
Hudson River 4, 7, 8, 10, 16, 19, 24, 29, 42, 44

immigrants 10, 11, 12, 13, 15, 18, 20, 24, 28, 32, 37, 44, 45, 47
Independence Day 38, 39
Intrepid Sea–Air–Space Museum 37

Irish community 5, 10, 11, 12, 16, 22, 38
Iroquois Native Americans 8, 44, 47
Islamic Cultural Center 23
Italian community 5, 10, 12, 22, 32, 33

jazz 4, 35, 41
Jewish community 5, 10, 12, 22, 23, 27, 31, 32, 33, 39, 42

King, Martin Luther 38

Latinos 5, 12, 13, 47
Liberty Island 6, 7
Lincoln Center 6, 7, 21, 34
Little Italy 6, 7, 12, 18

Macy's 30, 39
Manhattan 4, 5, 6, 7, 8, 9, 11, 12, 13, 14, 15, 16, 18, 19, 21, 22, 23, 24, 25, 27, 28, 29, 30, 31, 44, 45
Metropolitan Museum of Art 6, 7, 16, 36, 39
Minuit, Peter 8, 44
Museum of Immigration 6, 7
Museum of Modem Art 6, 7, 36, 42

Native Americans 8, 44
New Amsterdam 8, 9, 22, 44
New Jersey 6, 24, 29, 41
New Netherlands 8, 44
New York Aquarium 17
New York Public Library 42
New York State 4, 6

Olmsted, Frederick Law 16, 40

Parker, Dorothy 41
Pilgrims 39, 47
port 10, 24, 29, 37
Prohibition 27, 45, 47
Protestants 22, 47
Puerto Ricans 11, 13, 17

Queens 4, 6, 11, 17, 29, 45

Radio City Music Hall 34
Renwick, James 25
Rockefeller Center 6, 7, 25, 34, 38
Roman Catholics 22

St. Patrick's Cathedral 6, 7, 22, 23, 45
St. Patrick's Day Parade 12, 38
SoHo 6, 7, 19, 30, 36
South Street Seaport 6, 7, 24, 37, 39
sport 17, 35, 38, 39
Staten Island 4, 6, 11, 29, 39, 45
Statue of Liberty 5, 6, 7, 29, 45
Stock Exchange 25, 44
Strawberry Fields 19
Stuyvesant, Peter 9, 44

Tammany Society 11, 47
Temple Emanu-El 23
Theater District 6, 7, 34
Times Square 6, 7, 34, 39, 42
Triangle Shirtwaist Factory 24, 45
TriBeCa 19
Trinity Church 22, 44
Trump, Donald 45
Tweed, William Marcy 11, 26

United Nations 5, 6, 7, 47
US Courthouse 27

Vaux, Calvert 16, 40
Verrazzano, Giovanni da S, 44

Wall Street 6, 7, 9, 11, 25
Wall Street Crash 11, 25, 27, 45, 47
Washington, George 9, 14, 44, 47
Washington Square 17
World Finance Center 25
World Trade Center 4, 6, 7, 11, 15, 16, 19, 25, 27, 29, 45
World War II 11, 13, 31, 42, 47

Major World Cities

Prospect Heights Public Library
12 N. Elm Street
Prospect Heights, IL 60070
www.phpl.info